MADNESS OF WAR

-1973

PART I — MADNESS OF WAR

War as an event

PART II — UNFINISHED WAR

War as a State

A Book by Alex Avetis

"An unfinished war —
is a life that still goes on."

AUTHOR'S NOTE

This book is not a document and not a chronicle.
It does not attempt to explain war, nor does it try to
justify it.

I did not write about history or politics,
or about who was right or wrong.
All of that exists outside these pages.

I wrote about what remains after war —
about the silence that does not arrive at once,
about memory that does not disappear,
and about a person who continues to live
after the war has officially ended.

Madness of War (1973) is the story of a man
who entered a war and then tried to return from it.

The first part is a war that takes place outside.
The second is a war that continues within,
long after the gunfire has faded.

There is no clear boundary between them.
There is only a human being
trying to preserve himself, his memory,
and the ability to live on
without passing the war further.

Many scenes in this book are based on real experience.
Others come from an inner reality —
something that cannot be verified,
yet cannot be forgotten.

This is not a confession
and not a request for understanding.
It is a testimony — written not to accuse,
but to remember.

I did not write this book to transmit pain.
I wrote it to stop it here.

Many people carry war within themselves
longer than the war itself lasts.
They live among us,
and sometimes all they need
is someone willing to listen.

Because war truly ends only when it is no longer
passed on.

Alex Avetis

TABLE OF CONTENTS
Madness of War-1973

PART I
MADNESS OF WAR

War as an event

War doesn't always end with a gunshot.

Sometimes it ends inside.

Chapter 1. Before the War

"Sometimes life is still quiet,
but inside, the hum has already begun."

When Boris worked in the mine, life felt like a dark cage — noise, dust, vibration, sweat, and heavy air that settled in the lungs forever.

A mine dulls the mind. A man is left alone with himself, and if he does not keep his head straight, he becomes his own enemy.

Boris lived between shifts: down, up, eat, collapse into bed — and down again.

Days passed the same way. Weeks stuck together like the pages of an old book.

But inside him lived the feeling that he was stuck between two lives — the one that had already ended and the one that had not yet begun.

He had grown used to routine.

Yet beneath it, tension was always there — as if something were approaching, and he did not know what.

And then everything broke.

Chapter 2. Yom Kippur

"The loudest war
enters on the quietest day."

The Yom Kippur War began on October sixth, 1973.

As Israel sank into the silence of the holy day of Yom Kippur, as the streets emptied and people closed their shops to spend the day in prayer, the war entered the world like a heated blade.

The day when silence reigns in Israel — Yom Kippur, the most sacred holiday.

A day when even the air breathes slowly.

On that very day came the sound that tore the silence apart like a scream through prayer: the sudden attack of the Arab coalition. The strikes fell all at once — as if the sky itself had flipped over and begun to collapse.

Within hours, the country was descending into chaos.

Chapter 3. The Draft

"There are roads you do not turn onto —
you are led onto them."

Boris barely had time to understand what was happening when he was summoned to the draft office. From mining dust to military uniforms, a short path that no one chooses. He was mobilized immediately.

Around him were people just like him — silent, focused, as if they already knew there was no way back.

But no one knew that this war would turn Boris inside out so completely that he would stop recognizing himself.

Chapter 4. The White Ambulance

"Sometimes between life and death
there is only a steering wheel."

Boris was assigned to an ambulance — as a driver for a medical vehicle of the International Red Cross. His previous experience in emergency work saved his life... and at the same time destroyed it.

His task sounded simple and was impossible in reality: to evacuate the severely wounded from the battlefield to a hospital base. Sometimes under gunfire. Sometimes between exploding shells. Sometimes literally from beneath tank tracks.

It was a white, slightly worn vehicle. Inside, two stretchers were fixed along the sides, and two more were secured above — a maximum of four wounded at a time. Sometimes they transported five — when one no longer showed signs of life.

From the very first run, Boris understood that war is not noise, not screams, not fire.

It was a hum in the head that never fell silent.

He pulled people from mud, sand, from under rubble, under the whistle of bullets, under the roar of tanks. Sometimes he crawled. Sometimes he ran. Sometimes he stood over a wounded man and waited for the gunfire to subside.

He saw everything: blood, dirt, smoke, shrapnel. He saw people without arms, people without legs, people who were no longer here, though their bodies did not yet know it.

War revealed itself to him not as battle, but as an endless road — back and forth, between life and death.

And his mind began to change.

Because there are things a person cannot endure and remain the same.

Chapter 5. The Rule

"There are orders the body obeys.
And there are orders that break the soul."

There was a rule — rigid, written in the Red Cross instructions:

"If you are crawling toward a wounded man who is calling to you in your own language, you must crawl to him.

But if a wounded Arab lies nearby — you are obliged to take him first."

It did not matter what the heart said.
It did not matter what fury boiled inside.
It did not matter that someone you loved was fighting on the other side.

First — the enemy.
Then — your own.

Otherwise — a military tribunal.

It was humanity taken to the point of cruelty.

It was a war in which the human and the inhuman intertwined so tightly that no one could tell where the boundary lay anymore.

Boris listened to the instructions — and something inside him slowly began to crack.

He clenched his teeth.

Inside, everything burned.

But he obeyed.

Sometimes he crawled toward his own — those who shouted, "Brother, help me!" — and was forced to pass them by, to grab the shoulders of a bleeding, terrified man in a stranger uniform, speaking a foreign language, and drag him first.

It tore Boris apart from the inside.

But he did it.

He understood: a day would come when a fissure would open between the rule and his burning rage.

And it would break through.

Chapter 6. The Egyptian Front

"When the ground boils,
a person learns not to feel."

Boris was sent to the Egyptian front — one of the most brutal sectors.

The Egyptian front was different.

There, war did not hide. It moved openly — heavy, relentless, without pause. Tanks advanced like living creatures, without looking back. Aircraft tore the sky so low it felt as if, just a little more, and they would strike the ground with their wings.

The ground trembled constantly. Not even from explosions — from tension. The air was thick, as if metal had been dissolved into it.

Boris drove back and forth. Runs blurred together. Day, night — there was almost no difference. Sometimes he caught himself unable to remember how much time had passed: hours or days. War erases the calendar.

He pulled people from sand, from mud, from under rubble. Crawled. Ran. Waited for the fire to subside.

Sometimes he stood over the wounded and waited —
not for a doctor, but for a pause between shots.

He saw everything.

Blood.
Shrapnel.
Bodies still alive — but already not here.

And gradually he began to understand: if you feel all of
this, you will not survive. A person either dulls himself,
or breaks. Boris was dulling.

Chapter 7. A Friend

"There are people you change countries for.
And there are wars that take them away."

Boris had a best friend — like a brother.

They grew up together. Laughed together. Left
together. Dreamed together.

The friend left for Israel first. Boris followed — not
because of the country, not because of ideology.
Because of a person. He wanted to be near him again.
To visit him, sit at a table, talk about the future, about
a new life, about possibilities.

But on the very first day of the war, his friend was
killed.

That future no longer existed.

When Boris was mobilized, he already knew this. But knowledge does not arrive at all at once. The death of someone close is not news. It is a crack that appears inside and slowly spreads.

The friend served at the border. On Yom Kippur, soldiers had been sent home to celebrate. The strike came at that very moment — so sudden that many did not even reach their tanks. Some were crushed directly in the barracks.

This image haunted Boris, though he had never seen it before, he simply knew it had happened.

Chapter 8. The Closed Coffin

"A funeral without a body does not close death —
it opens emptiness."

Boris did not learn of his friend's death immediately. In the first hours of the war, information came in fragments. No one knew anything for certain. And in that uncertainty lived a strange hope: what if he is alive?

There were rumors. Talk of captivity. Pauses in which one could breathe, because the final point had not yet been placed.

Had Boris not been mobilized, he would have gone to search for his friend. Across the border. Under fire. Through anything. Because between hope and death there is sometimes only one step — and people still take it.

Then confirmation came. Brief. Without details. Killed on the first day. At the border.

And something inside Boris snapped.

It did not scream.
It did not explode.

It simply left — like air escaping from a punctured tire.

After that, he was no longer the same.

Chapter 9. The Brake

"Sometimes evil comes not as a blow,
but as a movement."

He continued to follow orders. He drove carefully, as before. Checked the stretchers, fastened the straps, watched the road.
But inside him a heavy, dense anger appeared. It did not shout — it lived.

It sat in his throat.
It rose to his head.
It did not let him sleep.

Sometimes, when a wounded Arab groaned in the back of the vehicle, Boris caught himself thinking that he did not care.

Sometimes — that he wanted the groaning to stop forever.

And these thoughts frightened him.

He knew they were wrong.

But anger did not ask permission.

War turns people into someone they never wanted to be.

One day he picked up a severely wounded Arab after a battle. The man was unconscious, strapped to the upper stretcher. The vehicle jolted over potholes. Dust hung thick in the air. Everything was routine.

But inside Boris that day, such fury boiled that he could not restrain it.

And he did something that a person does not do — something that the pain inside him did:

He slammed on the brake with a sharp movement.

So sharply that the wounded Arab tore loose from his stretcher, struck, and fell to the floor.

A wild scream burst from his chest.

Boris heard that scream — and froze.

And suddenly Boris felt... relief.

There was something in it...
something that, in a strange way, brought relief.

As if something hot that had been pressing from inside had loosened its grip.

As if the pain had finally come out — but not from him.

He felt warmth in his throat — as if thick smoke had escaped.

As if, for a second, the pain inside his very soul had fallen silent.

It was not him.

It was the beast that war had grown inside him in such a short time.

Chapter 10. The Russian Language

"War breaks where the enemy
speaks in your voice."

When Boris stopped the vehicle and began lifting the wounded man back up, fury churned inside him.

He started speaking — in Russian, so the Arab would not understand:

"You bastard... I hope you die... animal..."

He did not see a human being before him.
He saw an enemy.
The one who had taken his friend.
The one who had stolen his world.

And then — completely unexpectedly —

the Arab answered... also in Russian.

Hoarsely, with an accent:

"My friend... why are you angry with me?
Do you think I want to be at war? ...
I have a family. Children. I want to live.
If you refuse to go to war — we also face a tribunal.
I am the same person as you..."

Those words struck Boris harder than anything he had
seen before.

He had not expected Russian.
He had not expected truth.

He fell silent.

And for the first time in many days, a thought
appeared:

"Why am I angry at him?
He is not the one who killed my friend..."

He looked at the man — and for the first time saw not
an enemy, but a soldier. The same as himself. Trapped
between an order and life.

And at that moment, something clicked in Boris's
head.

For the first time, something inside him trembled —
something that would soon begin to collapse.

Chapter 11. Exhaustion

"A person holds on
until he stops sleeping."

Boris hardly slept.

His calls were endless: night — day — night again.

He was afraid to fall asleep, afraid to hesitate, afraid
to arrive too late for those who could still be saved.

Every time he transported people, he felt their lives
depended on his steering wheel, his hands, and his
attention.

Sometimes he fell asleep right on the hood of the
vehicle — under the open sky. Someone brought
mattresses, someone pillows. People set up tables with
food and water in the streets. The country helped itself
however it could, as if everyone had become one
family in hell.

Once, filthy and exhausted, he knocked on the door of
a random house.

"May I take a shower?"

They opened immediately. Gave him a towel. Fed him.
Packed food "for the road."

War kills —
but paradoxically, it sometimes reveals the best in
people.

And yet kindness could not stop the madness growing
inside him.

Chapter 12. The Hospital

"Sometimes the law is just,
but the world is not."

The hospital lived at the limit.

Beds stood pressed against one another. Corridors
were clogged with stretchers. The air was thick, heavy,
smelling of iodine, blood, and sweat. Doctors worked
without pause. Nurses fell asleep standing.

There were no enemies and no allies there.

There were only bodies.

Arabs lay on beds.
Israeli soldiers — on the floor.

Not because someone decided it that way.

There simply were not enough beds.

Boris saw this every day. And each time something
tightened inside him. He did not know what to call
shame, pain, or helplessness.

This is not forgotten.

It does not fit the mind of someone who sees his
friends die.

It seemed to him that the world had turned upside down: where there was love — there was pain; where there was duty — there was absurdity; where there was life — there was death.

And every time he wiped blood from the steering wheel of his vehicle, he felt no fear rising inside him — but a dull, heavy anger.

After another run, he felt his body no longer obey him. His head spun, his hands trembled. He blamed it on exhaustion and got back behind the wheel.

Chapter 13. The Explosion

"Some wars end suddenly.
The rest do not."

That day began like all the others — fatigue, the hum of the engine, a metallic taste of fear on the tongue.

Boris was driving along a dirty road, transporting the wounded — two critical, one serious, one barely conscious. All his attention was on the road. War teaches you: if you lose focus for a second, you are dead.

The road was empty.

The silence — suspicious.

And then — a sharp crack, dull, as if the earth itself had grabbed the air and crushed it.

Then an impact was so powerful that the world split into white and black.

A mine exploded beside the vehicle.

The ground surged up beneath him like a giant wave. The blast lifted the earth. The vehicle was thrown like a toy. The front slammed into the ground. Boris felt a sharp blow to his chest and pain in his leg as if it were clamped in a vise.

Two ribs — broken.
His leg — trapped between brake and gas.

Tearing pain shot through his body like electricity.

The world became muffled, as if submerged under water.

The cries of the wounded turned into distant sounds.

His head struck the glass — and everything vanished.

He lost consciousness.

Chapter 14. After

"To survive
does not mean to return."

He regained consciousness already in the hospital.

A white ceiling. A murmur of voices. The smell of medicine.

Bright lamps cut into his eyes.

Someone's voices sounded too loud.

He tried to rise — his body would not obey.

"Easy, easy..." a woman's voice said. "You have two broken ribs and a severe leg injury. You're lucky to be alive at all."

"Lucky."

What a strange word when there is emptiness inside.

Boris tried to ask:

"The wounded... what... what happened to them?"

But no one answered.

Or perhaps he simply did not hear — because consciousness slipped away again, as if someone were turning off the light inside his head.

For Boris, the war ended at that moment.

After the hospital, he walked heavily — as if the ground itself had become viscous.

He could not breathe deeply — his ribs hurt.

His leg ached constantly.

But worst of all were the looks he felt on the street.

When he began going outside, it seemed to him that people looked at him with judgment.

Why are you here?
Why not at the front?

No one knew that beneath his shirt were bandages.
That beneath his clothes were bruises.
That inside were fractures no one could see.

And those looks cut him more sharply than any wound.

He felt guilty — toward those who were still fighting,
and toward those who had died. Toward the friend
who was no longer there.

During war, a person lives on the other side of reality.

Afterward, he cannot return.

Chapter 15. The Return of Anger

"Anger is pain
that has no words."

Boris felt it: he was no longer the man he had been.

• He began to get angry for no reason.
• He flared up instantly.
• He lashed out if someone spoke even slightly
harshly.
• He felt constant, suffocating anxiety — as if an
invisible hand were gripping his throat.

At night he woke in cold sweat — hearing screams that
no longer existed.

He could not believe the war was over.

The body does not care.
The body keeps the war for a long time.

The anger did not leave. It became quieter — but deeper.

Sometimes he stood on the balcony for too long and looked down.

He wanted to drink and take a step forward — to be closer to his friend.

He thought:

"Maybe then I'll be closer to my friend?..
Maybe then the pain will go away?.."

But he stood. He held on.

Falling apart inside — holding together outside.

People told him:

"You need a doctor. You won't manage alone."

He did not go.

He thought he could handle it himself.
That time would heal.
That it would pass.

But time did not heal.

It only stretched the pain.

War does not let go so easily.

Chapter 16. The Drive

"Sometimes a person is not driving away from
something,
but toward a blow."

In Israel there is a road — long, straight, like a line of
fate.

From north to south.

The farther you drive, the more the signs, faces, and
intonations change. There are towns Israelis try not to
enter. Not because they are always dangerous, but
because they are always tense.

Arab cities within Israel. Jews usually bypass them to
avoid risk.

But one day — unlike the others — Boris felt as if he
was being pulled there.

Not by logic.
Not by desire.

By that dark, boiling rage inside him that he could no
longer contain.

He drove there like a man walking toward his own
destruction.

He did not think about what would happen next.

He wanted only one thing:

for the pain inside him to fall silent — if only for a second.

It was not a suicide attempt.

It was a desperate desire to feel a blow that would return him to reality.

He wanted to be free. At any cost.

The anger did not leave.

It lived in his chest like a clenched fist.

It demanded release.

Boris understood he was doing something foolish. He knew it could end badly. But at that moment, he did not care.

He was tired of carrying this pain inside.

Let them hit me.
Let them do anything.

Just let it end.

"I'm tired. I can't live like this."

Chapter 17. The Square

"The most dangerous places are
where life goes on."

But Boris drove straight there — as if obeying some dark force that does not ask, only demands.

He moved slowly through the center. Cars stopped. People looked. But no one shouted, no one rushed at him, no one tried to stop him.

People sat outside cafés, drank coffee, played backgammon, smoked, laughed.

The crowd was large but calm — ordinary life. Life went on as if there had been no war at all.

That made him even angrier.

He parked near the central café and got out.

All eyes turned toward him.

The only Jew in their quarter — it was visible at once.

And that calmness — that indifference — irritated Boris even more than if they had come at him with fists.

Several men sat at a table. One of them was especially big — tall, solid, with heavy hands. He tossed the backgammon dice, smiling lazily. When he was seated, they were almost the same height.

Boris walked up to them.

He looked the man in the eyes —
straight, cold, almost mad —
and said in a sharp, commanding voice:

"Stand up. Now."

The crowd fell quiet.

The man lifted his head. He did not understand what this young Jew wanted — alone, unarmed, in their neighborhood. He looked at him in surprise. He spoke Hebrew — like almost all Arabs living in Israel.

"What happened?" he asked.

Boris stepped closer, close enough to smell coffee and tobacco.

He struck his own cheek with his palm.

Not hard.

But hard enough for the sound to carry.

"Hit me," he said.

Chapter 18. Laughter

"Sometimes a blow heals better
than silence."

The Arab stepped back a pace.

He could feel something was wrong.

This man did not want to win — he wanted to be defeated.

"Are you crazy?"

"Afraid?" Boris's voice sharpened. "Hit me."

The crowd came alive.

Someone whistled.
Someone shouted, "Give it to him!"
Someone watched as if it were theater.

People began gathering around. They were curious.
Someone smirked.

"Look," someone said in Arabic. "Something's wrong
with his head."

The man stood up. At first cautiously. Then he hit Boris
— lightly, almost like a friendly slap.

Boris laughed.

"That's it?" he said. "You only stroked me with your
first hit, didn't you?
Come on, harder."

He shoved the man in the chest.

The Arab, now irritated, hit Boris again — harder.

Boris staggered but stayed on his feet.

And like a madman, he laughed.

"That's it! Better already!
More!"

He shoved the Arab again.

It was not a challenge to the man — it was a challenge to the world.

The smile disappeared.

"Enough," the man said. "Step back."

Boris shoved him again.

He was not provoking a fight.

He was provoking fate.

He was not drunk, not insane — he was broken.

And then the Arab, losing patience, struck with his whole body, his full weight, his full fury.

The third blow was real.

It was so strong that Boris's head snapped to the right, his body folded,
the ground swayed.

A hard, sharp hit — so hard that for an instant Boris's vision went dark.

The crowd stirred.

He fell — and in that moment he heard an explosion of laughter around him.

The crowd was laughing.
The Arab was laughing.
Everyone was laughing.

Boris raised his head.

Slowly — like a man returning from another dimension.

He looked around — and he himself…

he burst out laughing.

And suddenly — white light in his mind — he started laughing.

He laughed loudly, wildly, freeing.

As if something ancient and heavy had finally left him.

It was not laughter.

It was a scream that had finally found an exit.

And that laughter — shared, living, human —

broke the chain that had been pressing on him from inside.

The Arab who had been hitting him a moment earlier walked up and embraced him — tight, like a friend.

"You're strange," he said. "But brave. And… good. You're not an enemy."

Other men came over.

Someone patted Boris on the shoulder.
Someone held him by the elbow.
Someone said, "You okay, friend?"

People around laughed together with him.

They helped him get to his car.

Seated him behind the wheel.

They waved.

And Boris drove away —

and for the first time in many months, he felt

that it had become quiet inside him. Inside was empty.

But it was a good emptiness.

As if someone had switched off the noise of war in his head with a single hit.

The anger was gone.

Chapter 19. Silence

"There is an emptiness
in which you can breathe."

When Boris left the Arab town, he drove slowly, carefully, as if afraid to disturb the fragile silence that had settled inside him after the blow and the laughter.

The sun was already leaning toward sunset.

The road stretched along desert hills; the air smelled of overheated sand.

And for the first time in a long time Boris felt — not emptiness, not anger, not heaviness — but relief.

As if someone had turned a key inside him and opened a door that had been jammed for years.

He breathed deeply.

Watched the horizon.

And for the first time in months his breathing did not break, did not turn into a panicked jerk.

He understood:

he had returned.

Not completely.

But returned.

After that day, he never went back there again.

There was no need.

Something inside him had stayed there — on that square, among strangers faces, laughter, and a blow that proved stronger than any medicine.

He felt no victory.

No triumph.

He simply felt himself again.

That fight — absurd, risky, ridiculous —

became what neither doctors, nor IV drips, nor time had been able to do.

It returned Boris to life.

PTSD did not disappear completely — it never does. It is not an illness; it is a shadow.

But the weight lifted.

The hole stopped growing.

The anger left his body.

And now the shadow did not suffocate him — it simply existed somewhere nearby. It was there, but it did not control him.

He stopped jolting awake at night.

His hands stopped trembling when he heard a loud sound.

He began to look people in the eyes and see not threats but faces.

Slowly he began to return to his earlier self-esteem, the one he had been before explosions, before blood, before the loss of his friend.

But the wound left by his friend's death did not vanish.

It simply became part of his heart.

He felt he could live again as a man,

not as a shadow carrying war inside.

Nights grew quieter. Sleep still came with difficulty, but without that sticky anger that had kept his throat clenched.

Sometimes he woke from memories — from sharp sounds, from smells, from faces. But now he knew: it could be endured.

He shouted at people less. Stopped flinching at every word. Stopped searching for an enemy in every glance.

Often, he sat alone on a balcony or by a window — and thought of him.

Of the friend who had been like a brother.

Of the man whose fate had become part of Boris's.

Of how, if they had both survived,

life would have been entirely different...

Sometimes Boris caught himself feeling guilty:

Why did he survive, and the other did not?

Sometimes — in a silent conversation with his friend in his own head.

Sometimes — in a quiet tear he wiped away so no one would see.

But this grief no longer suffocated him.

Now it was light.

Like memory, not like a wound.

He no longer waited for him to return.

No longer built conversations in his head.

No longer argued with the past.

Only grief remained — clean, quiet, without anger.

Chapter 20. A Dream

"As long as a person can dream —
he is alive."

When everything settled,

when the body began to heal,

when nights became nights again and not nightmares,

Boris remembered that one thing remained that the war had almost taken from him:

his dream.

Once, before all of this, he had wanted to go far away. Very far. To a place that was cold and empty. Where there were no screams, no gunshots, no borders between "ours" and "theirs."

That distant place where, it seemed to him, one could begin life again.

Alaska.

Back then the dream had felt naïve.
Then unnecessary.
Then impossible.

Now it returned.

He did not know whether he would truly go.

He did not know whether it would work.

He did not know whether he would have strength.

But the very possibility of dreaming again meant one thing:

He had survived.

It is hard to live without a dream.

Without it life becomes mere motion — day after day, without direction.

He understood:

when a person loses his dream,

He stops living,

He only exists.

The war nearly took his dream.

But he took it back.

War takes much.

Sometimes almost everything.

But if after it at least one dream remains, then not everything is lost.

Conclusion

Boris sat on the top of a small hill, watching the sunset.

The sky was colored copper and gold.

Sand whispered under a light wind.

Boris thought:

"The most dangerous battle is inside yourself. And if you've won it — you're already a victor."

He did not consider himself a hero.

He did not think he had done something great.

But he survived.

He kept his heart.

He found his way back.

And that was the most important thing.

A war does not end on the day the shooting stops.

It ends when a person begins to feel alive again.

Boris went through what many go through — and what is rarely spoken aloud:

anger, guilt, shame, emptiness, the desire to disappear — and the slow return to oneself.

He did not become a hero.

He did not become an example.

He simply survived.

And that was enough.

The memory of the war remained with him — not as a scream, but as a scar.

A scar does not hurt every day, but it reminds you: it happened.

And it changed him forever.

But life remained as well.

The ability to look forward remained.

A dream remained.

And that means — the road continues.

PART II

UNFINISHED WAR

War as a State

"An unfinished war —
is a life that still goes on."

**"There are funerals that close a life.
And there are funerals that open an abyss."**

Chapter 1. The Day Announced Like an Order

"Some wars do not begin —
they continue inside."

The day of the mass funerals was announced the way a day off is announced. Dry. Bureaucratic. One line in the news — and half the country grew older by decades.

Cars streamed toward the cemetery. People drove in silence, pressing photographs to their chests, letters, scraps of clothing that still smelled of home. On the way no one spoke of the war — as if it could hear and return.

Beyond the gates, time was different. Not a day and not a morning — just light that did not warm. Women walked through it with white faces, and men whose eyes were somewhere far away, on that border where words ended.

Ambulances stood in rows, parked like witnesses. Medics had set up tents between graves in advance — as if they already knew the living would collapse more often than the coffins would be lowered.

Boris walked and felt the ground under his feet had become stranger — foreign. The cemetery path resembled a narrow hospital corridor: pain to the left, pain to the right, pain ahead — pain pretending to be order.

When they began lowering the first coffins, the air thickened. A hum rose around them — not the noise of a crowd, but one shared, heavy sound, like in a mine when a cart rolls along the rails and you hear it before you see it.

Then the wailing began. It did not belong to one person. It came from everywhere at once — as if the whole country were crying through mothers. And Boris understood: if that sound entered him, it would remain there forever.

At the entrance stood soldiers, young, with the same eyes the boys at the front had: adult eyes in a face that was too young. They did not know how to stand here. Simpleton everything is simpler — there is an enemy, direction, an order. Here the enemy was grief, and it had no direction.

Boris caught separate words: surnames, unit numbers, places of death. Everything sounded the same, like a list in a warehouse. And that made it worse: a human life was turned into a line so that the one reading would not go mad.

He noticed people clung to small things. To a purse strap. A coat button. The edge of a scarf. The hand of someone beside them. As if, if they let go of even one small thing, everything would collapse.

When a priest or an officer gave a speech, the words passed by. On that day, speech did not reach the brain. It settled somewhere in the chest like ash. And Boris felt his own chest tightening too, as if a stranger stone had been laid inside.

He understood then: a cemetery is not a place. It is a mechanism. It grinds a person slowly, quietly, and makes it so you go on living — but as someone else: smaller, quieter, more careful.

Chapter 2. Empty Coffins and the Absence of an Ending

"The past does not leave.
It only changes shape."

He watched them close the coffins. The lids came down heavy — but empty, without that finality that exists when you part with a body.

War has a particular cruelty: sometimes it leaves nothing at all to bury. It takes a person entirely, and in return leaves a form — like a shell — so that loved ones have somewhere to come and somewhere to place a candle.

Inside many of the coffins there was very little. Sometimes a cap. Sometimes a belt. Sometimes a piece of a uniform shirt. More often — soil from the field where the soldier died, so the box would not sound hollow.

And that was what drove people mad.

Because a funeral is not only memory. It is the last border. The last chance to say: here he is, here is the end, here—I let you go.

Here, letting go was impossible. Here they buried not a person, but a sign that he had existed. And the sign did not close the grief — it left it open, like a door at night.

That was how they buried his friend too. A closed box. No sight — no last look. Without a final "forgive me."

Boris stood, staring at the lid, and understood: they were asking him to put a period where his soul held a comma — and sometimes not even a comma, but a question mark.

When the box went into the ground, he felt not relief but collapse. As if something inside him had also been lowered — and covered with heavy wet earth.

Someone nearby whispered, "If only to see... if only one time..." — and that whisper was more terrifying than a scream. It sounded like a request in darkness when you already know there will be no answer.

Boris thought about how people in ancient times closed the eyes of the dead. It was a simple act: a palm, a touch, a final gesture. Here there was not even that. War stole the gesture and left only the box.

As they lowered his friend's coffin, Boris noticed his hands were shaking. He hid them in his pockets so no one would see. Men know how to hide a tremor. Women scream, men go silent — and inside them it becomes louder.

He wanted to remember his friend's face, but all he saw was the lid. Wood. Varnish. Nails. The smell of fresh boards. And that smell mixed forever in him with the memory of the man he loved like a brother.

Boris caught himself on an absurd thought: "What if we open it?" — and then understood at once that there was nothing to open. And that knowledge cut sharper than any truth.

When it was over and people began to disperse, the cemetery did not become quieter. It kept humming like overheated metal. And Boris understood: the vibration had settled in his bones.

Chapter 3. Nights of Searching

"Sometimes silence is more frightening
than any shot."

After the cemetery he stopped sleeping. Sleep is trust. And trust had been taken from him in a few days.

At night he would jolt awake as if by alarm and begin searching for his friend. He would feel the emptiness of the room with his hands, as if emptiness could be someone's back. He would listen to the silence — as if someone's voice might be hidden inside it.

Thoughts came in circles. What if he's in captivity. What if he's alive. What if he simply hasn't been found. And the most terrifying thought: what if I am sleeping calmly while he is somewhere waiting.

These thoughts gave him no rest. They were not logic — they were punishment.

Boris could sit by the window until morning, staring at the dark courtyard, waiting for someone to enter. Not because he believed. Because he could not wait.

They did not speak of post-traumatic stress then. Doctors treated the body the way they treat metal: straighten, stitch, bandage. No one knew how to bandage a soul.

And his war ended quickly — three or four days after his injury. But fear is not measured in days. It is measured by what you could not save. By what you lived through and could not forget.

His best friend died — and with him died a part of Boris that could not be buried, not even in a closed box.

By day he tried to behave normally. He smiled at acquaintances. Nodded to neighbors. Listened as people discussed prices, work, the weather — and did not understand how they could speak of the weather when yesterday, somewhere, they had buried earth instead of a Human.

He caught himself searching for his friend in crowds. On the bus. At the market. In the bread line. Every similar face struck his nerves like an electric shock: for a second his heart leapt, then fell back into emptiness.

Sometimes he imagined footsteps at the door. He would stand, go to open it — and behind the door there was nothing. Silence. The neighbor's corridor. And in that silence, he heard his own breathing, too loud.

He stopped trusting his body. The body could relax — and he would not allow it. He kept himself tense the way you hold a steering wheel on an icy road: let go, and you fly into the ditch.

The nights grew longer. Time stretched. Every minute became a separate room you had to leave, but the door would not open.

He began to understand that a person does not always die at once. You can keep walking, talking, eating — and still be half on the other side, where the closed box lies.

Chapter 4. The First Wave: Vodka and Earth

"A person comes back from war
not whole."

He had two waves of escape from this state. The first was short, like a breath in frost. The second stretched long, like a shadow behind a man in the desert.

He lost himself completely. It was a terrible time. And it was not only his soul that suffered — his grandmother suffered too. She did not understand war, but she understood the consequences: when someone is beside you, yet his eyes belong to someone who is already far away.

On the first evening he found a bottle of vodka and drank it all. He had never drunk before, and so vodka was not a habit. It was a tool. A way to switch off the light inside.

He fell to the ground, pressed his hand against it — and began talking to his friend. Not as to the dead. As to someone who had simply stepped into another room and would return any minute.

It seemed to him his friend answered. And to keep hearing that voice, he began drinking every day. Not for pleasure. For collapse. For that moment when consciousness gives up and the world turns soft like cotton.

He lay on the ground and listened to it. He could lie for hours. He vomited, he felt sick, because the body resisted while the soul demanded.

Drunk, he became dangerous. He could rush at people, shout into the sky: "Where is he? I want to know where he is!" — as if the sky were obligated to answer.

The first days of drinking were not celebration but work. He drank as a soldier follows an order: quickly, without taste, without enjoyment. The task was one — not to feel.

When he lay on the ground, he pressed his cheek to the cold ground and listened. It seemed to him a sound rose from the soil, like a distant conversation behind a wall. And he would have given anything for that conversation to become clear.

Sometimes he whispered, "Tell me you're alive…" — and answered himself: "You're insane." But the answer did not help. He drank again, to close the argument inside.

Neighbors began to avoid him. He saw them turn away when he walked up the stairs. He heard doors closing. And it made him angrier: it seemed the whole world had conspired to stay silent about the only thing that mattered.

His grandmother tried to speak to him, but he did not hear. He listened only to the earth. And that was the most frightening part: the living person beside him became background, and the dead became his main interlocutor.

One night he came to and realized he had been lying on the ground not for an hour — but for half the night. The sky was black, the stars motionless, and it seemed the world had paused, waiting for him to make a decision: to live — or to follow.

Chapter 5. The Shadow by the Bed

"Memory does not ask
whether you are ready to remember."

And it was after that that what changed him forever
began. He went through an encounter with the
Almighty. Not with his friend — with God.

One night Boris lay in his bed and stared at the ceiling.
The silence was thick. He was not asleep yet, but no
longer fully awake either. That in-between state is the
most dangerous. There, fears become objects.

In front of the bed, in the air, a silhouette appeared. A
huge cloak with a hood. There was no face. No eyes.
Only shadow. And the shadow was not standing on the
floor — it hovered, as if the air held it the way despair
held him.

Then he heard a voice. The voice did not come from
the silhouette — it sounded from all sides at once, like
in a movie theater when the speakers surround you
and you cannot tell where the sound is coming from.

The voice said, "What do you want? Why did you call
me?"

Boris answered honestly, because before such a voice
you cannot lie:

"I want only once to see my friend's eyes and
exchange two words with him."

The answer was calm:

"That is possible."

He was not frightened at once. First there was
surprise — as if the brain did not believe the eyes.
Then came the feeling that it was logical. That in his
condition could happen only this way: not through
people, but through shadow.

The silhouette did not threaten him. It simply existed.
And that was worse. A threat is an event; presence is a
law. You do not argue with a law.

Boris understood that he was speaking not with
someone who could be begged. It was like speaking to
the very mechanism of the world. As if you walked up
to a wall, and the wall suddenly answered.

When the voice said, "That is possible," Boris felt cold
under his ribs. Something inside him rejoiced — and at
the same time something understood you pay for
possibility.

He wanted to ask, "Why me?" — but did not. In that
moment he was no longer choosing. He had been
chosen.

The voice was calm, even slightly tired, as if it was not
the first time it had to explain to a human being that
death is not an ending, but a change of rooms.

And Boris felt that between his bed and the cemetery
there was no distance. There was only a thin partition
that could be crossed with a word.

Chapter 6. Instructions

"There is pain
that cannot be explained."

Then came instructions. Precise, like an order. And that made it even more frightening: God spoke as if it were ordinary business, as if such bargains were made every night.

"Take a bedsheet, two candles, and an alarm clock. Go to the cemetery where he is buried. Cover the grave with the sheet. Place the candles on each side. And most important — set the alarm clock for two minutes."

Two minutes. Only two. And it sounded like a sentence being counted down before an execution.

The voice warned: when the alarm rings, you may not want to switch places. If you do not switch — neither you nor he will ever have peace.

"You will be able to speak only once you have switched places. He will stand where you are. And you will lie where he is."

And the question that made Boris's hands go cold:

"Are you ready to come back when the alarm rings?"

He answered, "I am ready." Because in such moments a person answers not with the mind. He answers with pain.

When the words "switch places" were spoken, he imagined it not as a metaphor. He imagined cold earth under his back. The tightness. The weight. And for a second animal terror washed over him.

But immediately another wave rose — stubborn, furious: "If it is necessary, then it is necessary." Pain knows how to be brave. It is braver than reason.

He wanted to ask, "What if I do not make it in time?" — but the voice was already speaking further, as if any "ifs" were not accepted here.

He remembered the alarm clock most of all. Because an alarm clock is a human thing. Mechanical. Simple. And he was being asked to drive it into the mystical — like a nail into a cloud.

There was not a single word about forgiveness in these instructions. Not a single word about mercy. Only action. Like at the front: do this — you will survive. Do not do it — you will die.

When he said, "I am ready," he did not understand what he was promising. He thought he was promising risk. In truth he was promising himself whole.

And then prayer entered the room the way cold enters through an open window.

Chapter 7. The Cemetery

"Time moves,
but inside everything stands still."

Then the voice began to recite a prayer in a language
Boris did not know. It was not a conversational
language. It was the language of prayer — separate,
like a locked room in a house you can enter only on
your knees.

He understood nothing, but he remembered
everything. Each word settled into his head like metal
shavings: cold, sharp, forever.

When the prayer ended, the silhouette vanished. As if
it dissolved into the air. And Boris woke abruptly, like
after a fall.

He could not repeat anything consciously — but he did
everything as he had been told. He went to the
cemetery. The sheet. The candles. The alarm clock.

And when he stood before the grave and opened his
mouth, the prayer poured out of him — that same
prayer. Without effort. Without mistakes. He did not
understand a single word, but the words knew the
road by themselves.

Then the hum began.

The ground trembled. The air vibrated. Cracks spread
across the cemetery — not one, but many, as if
someone below were trying to pry open the lid of the
world.

Bodies began to rise from the ground. They were praying. With each word they rose higher and higher. Boris felt that his head was about to split. Only the final word remained — and at that moment he woke up.

The language of the prayer sounded as if it could not be spoken aloud in ordinary life. Each word seemed to catch the air and leave a scratch in it.

Boris tried to repeat it in his mind but could not keep up. The words flowed too fast, and he understood: memorizing it was impossible.

And then he understood something else: it would not be he who memorized it. Something inside him would remember — something that lives deeper than memory.

The cemetery was dark, but in the dream everything was visible. The candles burned evenly, as if the wind were afraid to touch them. The sheet lay over the grave — white on black earth, like a hospital cloth on a wound.

When the hum began, he felt it not with his ears, but with his teeth. His teeth trembled; his jaw tightened. The air became so dense it seemed you could suffocate from the sound itself.

The cracks ran through the ground like lightning. And each crack looked like a scar reopening.

The bodies rose slowly, as if the earth did not want to release them. They moved in prayer, swaying forward

and back, and Boris suddenly understood: this was not
only about him. It was about everyone. Everyone who
had not closed their goodbye.

The final word was like the edge of a cliff. He already
saw what lay beyond it — and woke up. He woke up
like someone both saved and cursed at once.

Chapter 8. Months of Repetition

"Sometimes life continues
in spite of you."

It was a dream. But it repeated every night. For
months.

Each time he reached the final word — and woke
before it. As if someone would not allow him to finish.
As if that word were a key that opened a door from
which you do not return.

By day, Boris lived like a man who had not fully woken
up. He walked the streets as if in a dream. He looked
at people and did not believe they were real.

It seemed to him that his real life began at night, when
he would again find himself in the cemetery. He waited
for night the way an addict waits for a dose, because
only there did his pain have shape and meaning.

He tried to prepare his head for the final word. He
wrapped it in towels. Made crude homemade clamps,

as if you could hold a skull together with iron when fear is splitting it from within.

He convinced himself he was not afraid that he would endure. But fear does not listen to persuasion. Fear lives on its own.

And each time — on the final step — he woke drenched in sweat, clutching his head as if he were truly holding it in his hands so it would not fly apart.

Sweat ran down his back, the sheet became wet, like after hard labor. He changed it every night, as if changing skin, but new skin did not save him.

He began to hate mornings. Morning did not bring relief — it brought the waiting for night. By day he was empty. By night he was filled with fear and purpose.

His thoughts narrowed to one thing: to finish the prayer. To say the final word. To reach the end. And the more he wanted it, the more his body resisted.

He tried sleeping during the day to trick the night. It did not help. Sleep came only when it wanted to, not when Boris did.

He thought he heard the alarm even in daylight. A phantom ring, thin as a needle. And each time it lifted a wave of panic inside him.

He began writing details of the dream into a notebook: where the candle stood, how the sheet lay, what sound appeared first in the air. He tried to turn madness into a map. Because a map means control.

But the map did not work. Because in that place of the world, control belonged not to a human being.

Chapter 9. When the Dream Became Life

"Fear does not disappear.
It learns to be silent."

Then the most dangerous thing began: he stopped understanding where dream ended and reality began.

He would wake, walk to the kitchen for water — and think it might also be a dream. He returned to bed and was no longer sure the bed was not a grave.

On the street he could approach a stranger and ask, "Pinch me. Harder. Hurt me so I understand where I am." People looked at him like a madman and stepped away.

Sometimes a thought came to him: make someone hit him. Provoke a fight. Let the blow be real — then he would know he was living, not sleeping.

He was frightened by these thoughts but could not stop them. War teaches you: when everything inside is burning, you search for any cold.

He lost his sense of time. If someone asked whether it was day or night, he could not answer. He could sit by the window and wait for an alarm that was not there.

And his grandmother saw all of it. She held the house the way you hold up a ceiling that is about to collapse: with hands, nerves, prayers.

He began to confuse faces. A doctor could seem to him like an Arab from the ambulance. A neighbor could seem like a soldier from the front. Any word could become a signal for alarm.

Sometimes he caught himself speaking out loud in an empty room. He told his friend what he had not managed to say. And it seemed to him someone was listening. Then he understood it was himself listening to himself — and it became even more frightening.

He stopped eating normally. Food had no taste. The only taste was water after a night of sweat — water was proof the body still worked.

Boris could stand in front of a mirror and not recognize the gaze. The eyes were his — but not his. There was too much night in them.

He began to fear silence. Because silence was the same thing that existed before the silhouette appeared. And every time the room became too quiet, he waited for the shadow to come again.

At some point he understood he might cross a boundary by accident. Not on purpose. By accident. Simply one day does not return from the dream. And that thought became another alarm clock ringing inside.

He held on to his grandmother with his eyes. To her hands. To her habit of putting the kettle on. To her quiet prayers. She was his last thread to life, though she did not know it.

Chapter 10. Grandmother and the Doctors

"The hardest roads
are the ones back."

His grandmother took him to doctors. She believed in people in white coats because there was nothing else left to believe in.

The doctors listened but did not understand. He tried to explain that every night he almost spoke the final word that could exchange places between the living and the dead. That his head could not withstand it. That he lived inside a dream.

They prescribed medications. Sedatives. Sleeping pills. Something "for the nerves." They treated symptoms because they did not know the cause.

Boris did not care. He wanted only to return to bed sooner, to see the dream again. To come again to the last word. To try again to finish.

Sometimes he thought: maybe it was punishment. Not for vodka. Not for screaming. But for the fact that he remained alive while his friend went away.

Sometimes he thought: maybe it was a test. But a test of what? His will? His faith? His desire to die?

His grandmother sat beside him and said nothing. She could not enter his dream, but she could hold his hand so he would not go too far.

The doctor's office smelled of alcohol and paper. To Boris that smell resembled the frontline hospital, and he began to shake.

The doctors asked questions: "When did it begin?" "Do you sleep?" "Do you drink?" — and in those questions he heard not care, but an attempt to put him into a frame. And he did not fit. He lived between the grave and the bed.

His grandmother argued with the doctors, demanded explanations. She said, "He's a good boy. He just lived through a war." In those words was everything: love, fear, helplessness.

Sometimes the medication gave him a few hours of heavy sleep without dreams. He woke and felt robbed: they had taken from him the night in which he was trying to finish the prayer. He grew angry even at relief.

He did not want to be a "patient." A patient is someone treated. And he believed they were not treating him — they were waiting to see whether he would break on his own or manage on his own.

At night his grandmother sometimes rose and checked whether he was breathing. She did it quietly, like a

thief. Because she was afraid that one day he would
not be breathing.

Boris saw her fear and felt guilt.

But guilt does not heal.

Guilt only makes the night darker.

Chapter 11. The Speedometer

"A person is not exhausted by events,
but by their echo."

One day a simple thought arrived. Not a prayer. Not a
sign. Just a thought:

If in the dream he drives to the cemetery, that means
he gets into the car and drives. Which means in the
morning the car should not be standing where it stood.
And the speedometer should show something different.

He wrote the numbers on a scrap of paper before
sleep. The way an accountant records the cash drawer
to check in the morning whether someone stole it.

Waking at night, he would go for water and
immediately go downstairs — to check the car. To
check reality.

The speedometer did not change. The car stood in
place. The slip of paper matched the numbers.

And for the first time in a long time Boris smiled briefly, without joy, but with relief:

So, it is a dream.
So he is still here.

He began to trust not people and not words. He began to trust metal. Because metal does not fantasize and does not confuse worlds.

After a few nights he stopped wrapping his head. He told himself, "I'll try again. If it splits — let it."

And suddenly — nothing happened.

He simply fell asleep.

And woke in the morning.

No dream. No humming. No cemetery.

Silence came quietly — and that made it even more frightening.

The speedometer thought did not arrive as revelation, but as exhaustion — when exhaustion becomes so strong that the mind clings to the simplest thing just to survive.

He began to write down not only the numbers but the position of the car as well: where the wheels were turned, how close it stood to the curb, how the lamp reflected in the glass. He took a photograph with his eyes so he could compare in the morning.

Checking the car became a ritual. He woke, drank water, then went downstairs. The cold hallway air hit his face. The car's metal was cold, real. He touched it with his palm the way you touch something alive.

Each time the numbers did not change, he felt he returned by a millimeter. Not a step — a millimeter. But millimeters add up into a road.

He began to allow himself small things: to eat normally, to go out into sunlight, to speak to someone without thinking it was a dream. These were tiny victories over the night.

And one day he slept and woke up in the morning without a dream.

At first, he was afraid. An empty night is frightening too. Because emptiness reminds you of a closed coffin.

But then he understood:

Silence is also life.

Just a different kind.

Quiet.

Careful.

Chapter 12. The After-Silence

"Forgiveness does not always come.
Sometimes acceptance comes."

From then on, the dream never returned. There was no final word. There was no exchange of places. There was no meeting.

From the whole story one question remained: how could he recite the prayer without understanding a single word? The words lived inside him separately, like fragments of shrapnel that were never found, never removed.

Another fear remained as well: that the dream could return. Not even at night — in daylight, suddenly, the moment he relaxed and forgot he had once stood on the border between two worlds.

His friend no longer came. He stayed in Boris's heart — in the place from which he would never leave. The friend became part of his breathing: inhale — memory, exhale — guilt.

Boris sometimes caught himself avoiding thoughts about that night. Because thought is a door. And he did not want to find himself standing before it again.

He repeated a simple phrase to himself: in everything truly brilliant there are simple things. And what returned him to life was not an angel and not a vision — it was the speedometer. A small scale with numbers. A simple anchor for a man who was drowning.

And yet the war did not end completely. It merely learned to be silent. And silence can be more frightening than gunfire.

He tried to remember the final word of the prayer, but it did not come. As if it had been withheld on purpose, so he would not open the door.

Sometimes he thought: perhaps that was mercy. Not to let a person do what he begged for in despair. Because despair asks badly — it asks for death, believing it is asking for peace.

Years later he was still afraid to remember. Afraid even to tell the story. Because telling is repetition. And repetition could become a summons.

But the memory of his friend was not a summons. It was a quiet room inside his heart, a room he entered rarely and carefully — the way you enter the room of the dead, so you don't touch their things.

In his mind he said, "Forgive me, brother." And added, "I couldn't come to you then." And in those words, was everything that remained of that war: guilt, love, helplessness — and some stubborn life.

He was saved by simplicity. The speedometer. Numbers. Metal.

There was a strange truth in that: sometimes what returns a person to reality is not a miracle, but an instrument panel.

But the war still stayed inside him. It had simply learned to keep quiet. And silence is also a sound. You just hear it only at night.

Chapter 13. A Ban on Memory

"There are losses
that become part of your name."

Weeks passed, then months. The dream did not return,
but its shadow lived nearby — like a memory of pain
that could wake again.

Boris learned to pretend everything was normal. He
left the house, worked, and spoke to people. But inside
he kept one rule: do not come too close to that door he
had almost opened.

He avoided cemeteries. Avoided candles. Avoided
alarm clocks that rang too sharply. Any ring could
become the first blow to his nerves.

Sometimes on the street someone said the word switch
— and his spine went cold. He smiled, nodded,
continued the conversation, while in his mind he saw a
white sheet on black earth.

At night he listened to silence. Not to sound to the
absence of sound. Because the shadow came precisely
when everything grew too quiet.

He began to understand: memory is not an archive. It
is a minefield. You can walk for years, and nothing
happens — and then you step on one single sound, and
everything explodes again.

So he forbade himself to think. Forbade himself to dissect that night. Forbade himself to seek explanations. An explanation could become a thread leading back into the abyss.

But a ban does not erase. It only pushes deeper. And sometimes Boris felt: beneath the ban, a question lived. It did not shout. It simply waited.

The question was simple and terrifying:

Who spoke to him — God, his mind, or the war that had learned to speak in prayer?

He did not try to answer.

Because an answer might be more dangerous than not knowing.

Chapter 14. Kitchen. Grandmother

"Sometimes you have to reach the edge
in order to stop."

One evening his grandmother sat beside him in the kitchen. The kettle hissed like a small engine. Bread lay on the table, untouched. Food was only a pretext to gather in one place.

She was silent for a long time, then spoke quietly, as if afraid that someone third would hear her words:

"I saw you leaving life while you were still here."

Boris lifted his eyes. He wanted to say something intelligent, grateful, grown-up. But only air came out.

"I was afraid," she continued, "that one day you wouldn't come back."

"Not from a dream. From everything."

Her hands were trembling. Not from age — from having held the house on herself for too long while it was falling.

And Boris suddenly understood: his madness had not been only his. It had been shared. His grandmother had lived inside it with him — only without visions, without prayers. She lived in the waiting that his body would remain, but he would be gone.

He said, "Forgive me."

And that word was the only one he could say honestly.

His grandmother nodded. She did not want explanations. She wanted only one thing: that he would be here. That his breathing would be heard in the morning.

That evening, for the first time, he allowed himself to cry.

Not like a child.

Like a person who had held his face too long while everything inside collapsed.

Chapter 15. A Letter to a Brother

"Not every wound closes.
Some simply stop hurting."

That night he did not sleep. But now it was a different insomnia — not panic, not waiting for the dream, but a quiet, even pain.

He took paper and sat down to write a letter to his friend. Not to send it. To finally say what he had not said over the closed coffin.

"Brother, forgive me that I did not see your eyes one last time. Forgive me that there was no farewell. I stood over the lid and felt that I was burying not you — I was burying a hole inside myself."

He wrote slowly. Each sentence came out like blood from a wound — not because there was so much of it, but because it was real.

"I searched for you at night. I thought about captivity. I thought you were waiting. I couldn't allow myself to sleep. I tried to speak to the earth as if the earth were a telephone."

He stopped, placed his hand on the page, and understood: he could hear that hum again. Not a real one — a remembered one. The hum of the cemetery. The hum of cracks. The hum of prayer.

He continued:

"If there is a place where you can hear — know this: you live in me. Not as pain. As a compass. As the thing that keeps me from falling."

He finished:

"I don't know who came to me then. God or war. But I know something else: I stayed. I did not exchange places. I did not leave. Maybe that is cowardice. Maybe it is mercy. But it is my life. And I will carry you in it until I meet you where alarm clocks are not needed."

He folded the sheet, hid it inside a book, and turned off the light.

And for the first time in a long time, the darkness in the room did not feel like an enemy.

It was simply darkness.

Without a silhouette.

Chapter 16. The Silence That Arrives

"An unfinished war
is a life that still goes on."

An epilogue is never a period. It is a line you draw yourself — so you do not return to the place where the earth speaks to you.

Boris sometimes caught himself still counting sounds. A loud door slam — like a gunshot. Heels on the stairwell — like the steps of a guard detail. The telephone ringing — like an alarm set for two minutes.

But now he knew: sound is only sound. And if you manage to name it in time, it won't become a vision.

He learned to live by small habits. Morning tea. Keys in the same pocket. A note on the table. Simple things held him more firmly than big words.

Sometimes he still drove past the cemetery and felt cold rise inside him. He did not turn his head. But in his mind he said, "I remember." And that was enough.

War took from him faith in calm sleep.

But it gave him something else: the understanding that a person survives not by heroism. He survives by anchors.

His anchor turned out to be the speedometer. Numbers on a dashboard. Nothing holy. Nothing beautiful. Just proof that reality remains in place — if you yourself have not driven anywhere.

Sometimes he thought: perhaps that was the mercy. He was not given the prayer's final word — he was given a simple way to check the world. Not a door into death, but a handle on the door back.

And when he remembered his friend, he no longer searched for him in the earth. He searched for him inside himself — in the way he kept his word, in the way he did not strike the weak, in the way he did not let the beast of war grow inside again.

Because an unfinished war ends only in one way: when you stop passing it on.

And then silence truly comes.

Not at once.

But it comes.

EPILOGUE

What Remains

This book does not close the war.
It only shows where the war ends
inside one person.

This book ends,
but the story does not end the same way.

War knows how to leave without goodbye.
It can vanish from the news,
from conversations — and remain inside a person
as a quiet noise within silence.

I joined these two parts not to put a period,
but to draw a line: where war ends
and where the return to oneself begins.

If there is pain in these pages —
it is not here so it can be passed onward.
It is here so it can stop here.

So that memory does not become a weapon.
So that another person's death does not become
an excuse for new cruelty.

Memory remains.
But with time it can stop being a sentence
and become responsibility:

to protect the living,
not to be ashamed of tears,

not to demand a quick return from yourself,
not to let darkness speak instead of the heart.

If a reader recognized themselves in these pages —
it means they are not alone.

If after reading, it becomes quieter inside —
it means this book was needed.

Sometimes that is enough.

ISBN: 979-8-9949132-4-6

Author's edition.

Printed in the United States of America